BUSTER

by Linda Jennings

illustrated by Catherine Walters

WHEN Buster was eight weeks old he had to leave his mother and go off to a new home. He was a bit sad at first, but he soon cheered up. His new family kept cuddling him and calling him cute.

As Buster changed from a puppy into a proper little dog, things began to go wrong. He tried his best to please, but he didn't know that some human beings love small cuddly puppies, but can't stand full-grown dogs who lick your face and chew things up.

"Dratted dog!" they shouted. "More trouble than he's worth!"

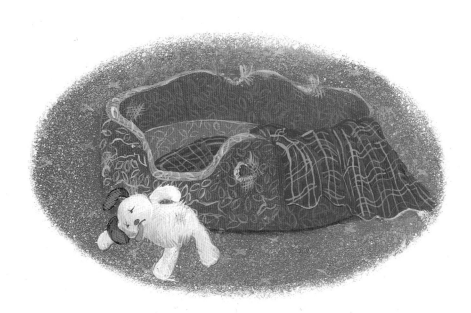

ONE cold winter's day, his owners took Buster to
a part of town where he had never been before.
There they pushed him out of the car and left him on
the edge of a wide busy road.
They didn't want Buster any more.

THE cars raced by all day, and nobody noticed poor Buster. It grew dark, and the car headlights shone like huge, fierce eyes. Buster was very frightened. He wanted to go home – but where *was* home?

WITHOUT thinking, Buster rushed out into the road. SCREECH! CRASH! Two cars braked to avoid him, but hit each other. Two furious heads leaned out of two wound-down windows and yelled at the little dog.

The angry voices made Buster think of the family who had abandoned him.

SCRE ECH

HE fled into a garden and lay trembling under a laurel bush. When his heart had stopped thumping, Buster came out. It was cold, very cold, and he was hungry. He crept up to the closed front door of the house, and scratched at it.

THE door opened, and a woman peered down at Buster. But before she could say anything, a huge snarling dog appeared from behind her, and thrust its head into Buster's face.

"Clear off, before I bite you!" he growled. "This is *my* home."

BEFORE Buster could move, the big dog broke free, and chased him right down the garden path, snapping at his short stumpy tail. Buster just managed to squeeze through a hole in the hedge before the big dog could attack again.

BUSTER sat on the frosty pavement, licking his sore tail. Where should he go now? He trotted on, and hesitated at another open gate. There were a lot of lights sparkling from a tree in a window. The house looked very cheerful and welcoming.

BUSTER started to walk up the drive, but he didn't get far.

"Push off, Blackeye!"

Buster looked up. Sitting on the wall above him was a large tabby cat.

"My territory," he hissed. "Gerroff." The cat flexed his claws and opened his mouth, showing a set of sharp, white teeth.

"OK," sighed Buster, "I'll go."

"NOBODY wants me," thought poor Buster. It started to snow, and Buster's fur grew wetter and wetter. His little body shook with the cold. Some people were walking down the road, singing. If he could move along with them, they might notice him, and take him home. Keeping well behind, he followed them, in the shadow of the hedge.

THE singers turned into a driveway. "Silent Night, Holy Night," they sang, as they stood in a circle outside the house. Buster crept among them, wondering if they would notice him, and half hoping they wouldn't.

THE door opened, and Buster could smell something delicious. He dribbled with hunger.

"One for each of you," said a voice, and a hand held out a plate of mince pies.

"Thank you, Mr. Merrydew," said the carol-singers.

"And one for the little dog," he added.

THE little dog? Everyone turned round, and then looked down at their feet. Buster gazed up at them, hunger pleading in his eyes. Would they tell him to go away, too?

"Who is he? Where has he come from?"

"He must be a stray. He looks very hungry," said a small girl, and she gave Buster a whole mince pie. He swallowed it in one gulp.

OLD Mr Merrydew came out of the house and looked at Buster. A dog for Christmas! No, not just for Christmas. A dog for life!

"I'll take him," he said. "It looks like he needs a good home." He put out his hand to Buster, and the little dog drew back, afraid.

"Come on, little fellow," said Mr Merrydew gently. "We'll have a good Christmas together, you and I."

BUSTER lay stretched out in front of the fire, his tummy full and warm at last.

"Happy Christmas, little dog," said Mr Merrydew, "and welcome to your new home."

"Woof!" said Buster.